D0183423

First published in Great Britain by HarperCollins Children's Books in 2008

10 9 8 7 6 5 4 3 2 1

ISBN-10: 0-00-727523-4 ISBN-13: 978-0-00-727523-6

A CIP catalogue record for this title is available from the British Library.

The HarperCollins website address is: www.harpercollinschildrensbooks.co.uk

Based on the television series Roary the Racing Car and the original script
'Green Eyed Roary' by Chris Parker.

Visit Roary at: www.roarytheracingcar.com

Printed and bound in China

Green Eyed Roary

HarperCollins *Children's Books*

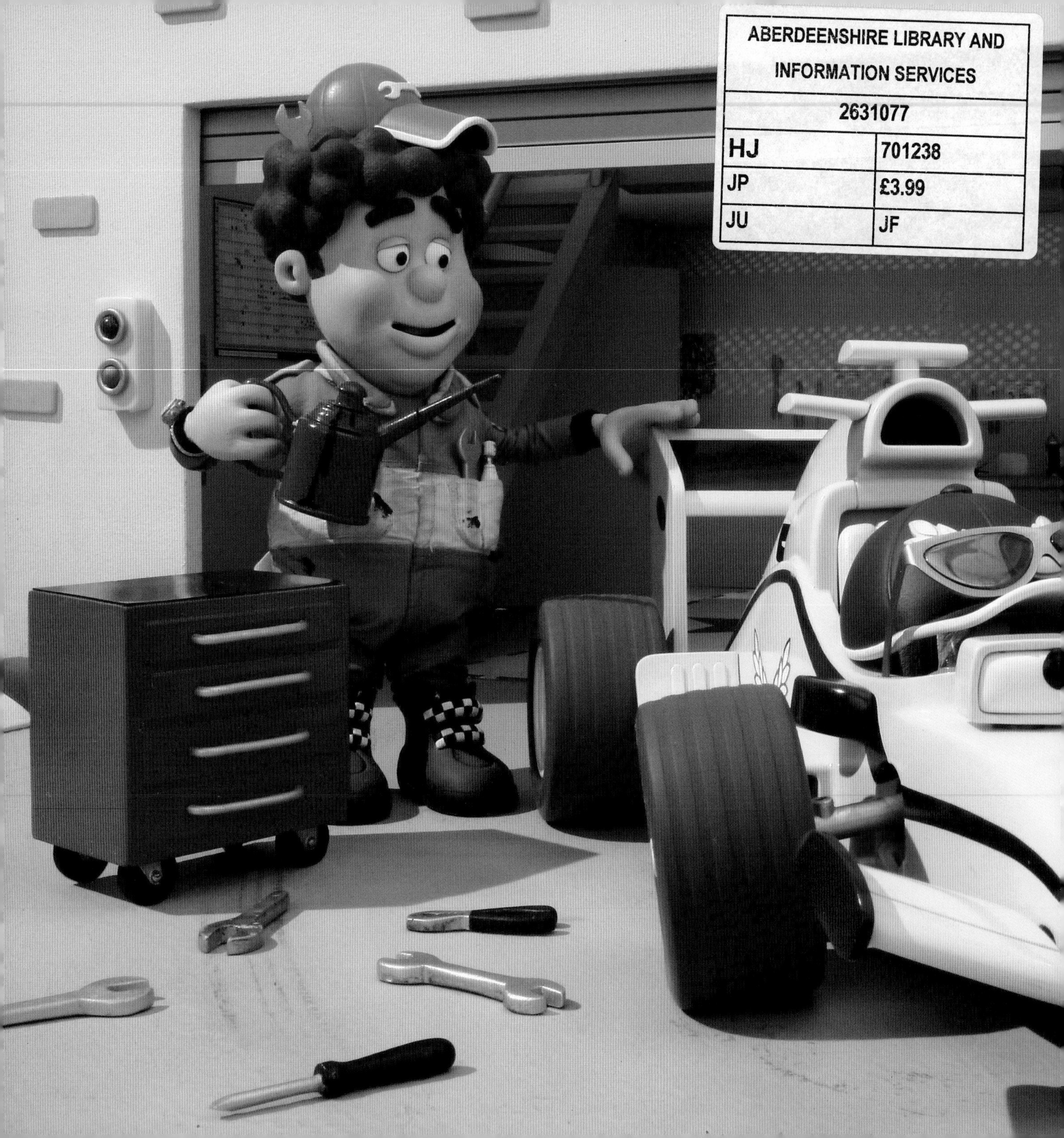

Big Chris had been tuning up Maxi's engine.

"Now all you need is a training partner, Maxi, and you'll be able to get back into tip-top condition!"

"Ha ha!" laughed Maxi. "Which of the other cars is brave enough to train with me?"

Cici jumped at the chance to train with her hero, Maxi!

"I'll do it, Maxi," she said quickly.

Roary was surprised that Cici wanted to train with the racetrack showoff, Maxi! But Big Chris just smiled, and said, "All right, Cici. Off you both go, then. Once around the track for a warm-up."

"My engine needs a tune-up, too," said Flash, as he zoomed around Big Chris in circles. "Could you take a look at it for me?"

Maxi and Cici forgot that Big Chris had told them to do a warm-up lap. They raced as fast as they could. Maxi was impressed.

"You're good, Cici!," he said as they arrived in the pit lane. "I don't know why you hang around with that little squirt, Roary."

Cici wanted to defend Roary. But she also wanted Maxi to like her. "Well, I suppose he can be a bit childish sometimes," she said, then quickly changed the subject. "Shall we go around again?"

But Cici didn't know that Roary had just come into the pit and had heard everything that they had sent.
Roary was very upset. He watched as his best friend raced off with Maxi. Just then, Tin Top arrived.

"What's the matter, Roary?" he asked.

"Oh, it's Cici," said Roary, sighing.

"I thought you two were best friends," said Tin Top.

"Hmm," said Roary, "I think she's got a new best friend now." Tin Top understood straight away. Roary was jealous.

Big Chris had finished working on Flash's skateboard. "Well, I guess I should really give it a test run," he thought to himself. But he'd never ridden a skateboard before.
He was only on it for a few seconds before he fell off!

"Hmm," he said to himself. Then, "I'm not going to let this beat me!"
But he looked around to make sure no-one was watching before he got on it again.

Cici was really enjoying herself with Maxi.

"Training with you every day is going to be great," she told him. Maxi wasn't so sure. "Every day?" he thought. Maxi was beginning to get tired of Cici.

"Actually, I'm feeling a little tired," he said, "I think I'll go back to the workshop for a polish."

"Ooh," said Cici, "I love it when your paintwork is all shiny. I'll come and watch in case Big Chris misses a bit."

"Er… you don't need to go everywhere with me, Cici," said Maxi. Cici was upset.

Back at the workshop Roary was upset too.
"How about that race now, Roary?" Cici asked.
"I thought I was too childish for you," he said.
"Why don't you go and race Maxi instead?"

Cici realised immediately what must have happened. She felt silly for trying to impress Maxi. But mostly she felt bad about having upset her best friend.

Big Chris was getting a little better at skateboarding, and just beginning to enjoy himself when Tin Top arrived to tell him about Roary and Cici. While he was listening, though, Big Chris accidentally stepped on the engine block, and suddenly he was zooming off out of control! He zoomed right past Cici, and then Roary.

“Hold on, Big Chris,” said Roary, anxiously, “I’m coming after you!” and off he roared.

“Oh la la,” said Cici, “Roary needs my help,” and off she roared after him.

The cars soon caught up with Big Chris.
"Big Chris," called Roary. "Jump on to my bonnet!"
But Big Chris didn't want to jump.
"I might miss..." he yelled. But Cici joined in.
"Come on, Big Chris, jump! Roary will catch you," she called. Finally he did – and just before the skateboard crashed into the tyre barrier!

Soon they were all safely back at the workshop.
"Thanks, you two," said Big Chris. "You know, my whole life flashed in front of my eyes when I was on that skateboard! I don't know what I'd have done without you! Now, what's this problem Tin Top said you needed to talk to me about?"
Roary and Cici smiled at each other.

"Oh, it's nothing, Big Chris," said Roary. Then he turned to Cici and said, "How about once round the track?" Cici smiled. "What about the rest of you?" Roary continued, and soon all the cars were enjoying themselves racing around the track.

"Fancy another go, Big Chris?" asked Flash.
"You can hop on behind me if you like."
"No chance," said Big Chris firmly. "I'm sticking to cars from now on! Cars and tea, that's me... oh, and biscuits. Mustn't forget the biscuits." And, smiling happily, he dunked a biscuit in his tea.

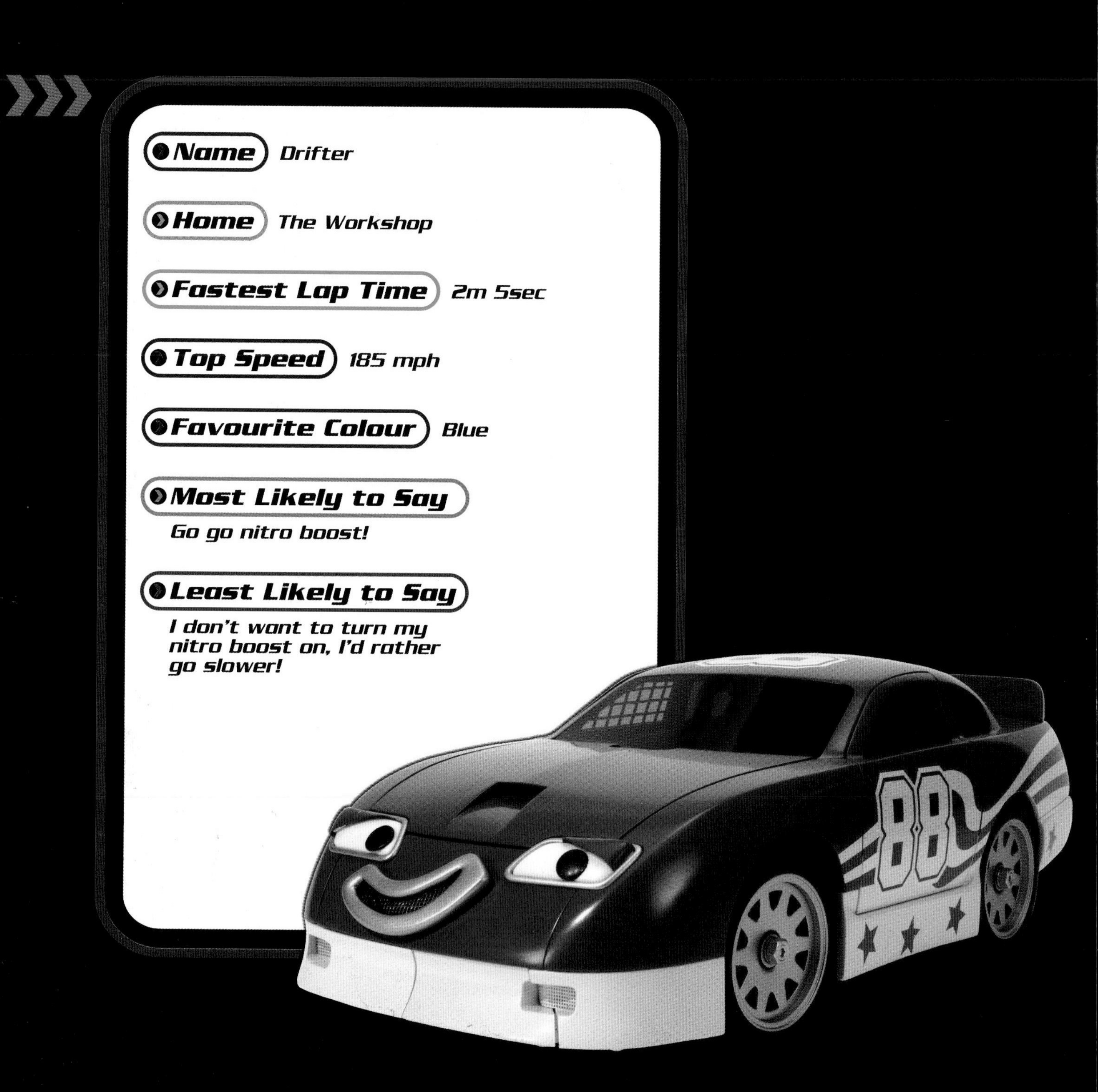

Name Drifter
Home The Workshop
Fastest Lap Time 2m 5sec
Top Speed 185 mph
Favourite Colour Blue
Most Likely to Say
Go go nitro boost!
Least Likely to Say
I don't want to turn my nitro boost on, I'd rather go slower!
88

Tin Top
88
88
88

ROARY® The Racing Car

Race to the finish line with these fun story and activity books.

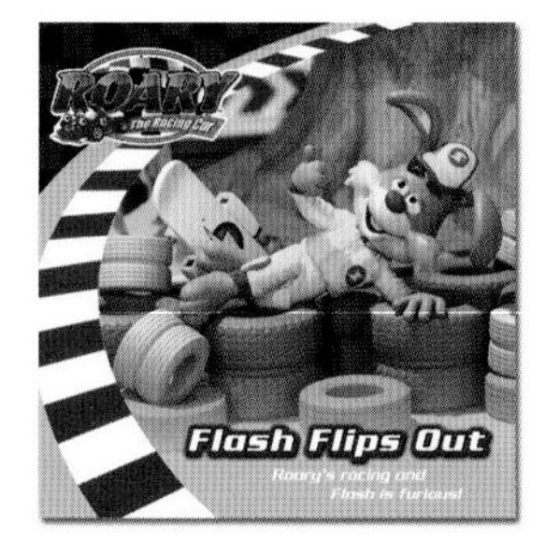

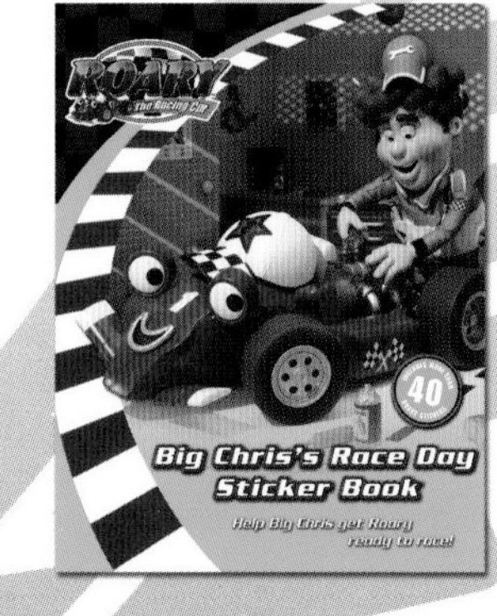

Roary the Racing Car is out soon on DVD!

Rev up R/C Roary to race to victory!

Start your engines with Talking Big Chris!

Go Roary, go-oooo!

Get ready to race!

Light 'em up Roary!

Visit Roary at www.roarytheracingcar.com

As seen on TV milkshake!

As seen on Nick Jr.